Street Wars: Beginnings and

Street Wars: Beginnings and Endings by George H. Clowers, Jr. 3rd Edition

Cover Art by Deborah A. Clowers

Honest deceptions, a recovered life, and good outcomes for people who know how to use street cred in the boardrooms!

The evening clouds were darker today, mid-December, looking from the bathroom window to the west, the tint of red diminished to a few streaks interspersed amongst them. Celia and Leroy were glad to be back home, though they had a good visit with Jake's family up north. Jake and Leroy had completed their initial business plan for H.U.N and would fly to San Francisco after the King holiday. Leroy was adjusting to a more formal presence as he would be dealing with accountants, lawyers, and consultants from prestigious schools, and wouldn't need to show his street cred, only his intelligence. Oddly, it would be Jake who had to present street credentials to back up his clean-cut image. Cynthia Tucker, H.U.N.'s founder, had every confidence in his abilities to steer her company in the right directions, even though these would be broader markets than he was accustomed to. The money would be larger as well, but Jake was seen as a player by tech industry financiers and would have no problem mingling with the billionaire crowd. Some had known Wallace Henson and were comfortable that Jake knew his way around the table.

*

Randall Brewer suspected Leroy Fleming was responsible for Bruce Walker's death. Not many ex-cons, or soon to be cons, had the juice to pull that off. It was known in certain circles that Leroy was still angry about his friend's murder back in 1995. Bruce, and Thomas Robinson, in their undercover roles, considered it just another day at the office, and helped the press report that it was probably 'gang related.' Reality was, the guy was just greedy, not a threat, another dope fiend trying to get a little more out of a deal. They could have cuffed him, taken him in, and questioned him until he rolled over on a few folks. Information about who was moving how much was what they were after, or so Leroy thought.

*

While Leroy traveled, Celia would teach a master's level class in painting for two months. Late January and most of February were her most creative times of the year, and she would be laser focused on whatever work was in front of her. She looked forward to developing this course for promising, under exposed students who lived on the other side of the tracks, literally, but had done adequate undergraduate work, and had enough promise to become serious artist, or at least could develop skills on how to earn a living as an artist. Whichever, Celia was excited about the coming year and had plans to stay busy the few times Leroy would have to travel for business. She was glad to have time again for art.

She thought back to the last time she was in San Francisco, the summer of 1997, and her walks from the Art Institute back to Fisherman's wharf. She loved the aroma and fragrance of China Town, and the visual of the hills as they slowly flattened the closer you got to the pier, then the skyward call of the residences across the bay. Lombard Street was fantastic, the flowers shouting their colors, the freedom she felt there, and how her creative 'wiggles' would come together at the Museum of Modern Art and the galleries along Third Street; even the homeless man who slept in the doorway near her hotel seemed to add a sense of specialness to it all.

She could retaste the Red Snapper lunch she had with her sister Delia, and see the sculptures in front of her yard, and even the bird house made of glass, mud, and twigs set between two trees at the side of the house. Delia was a free floater, unencumbered by the rules of convention, only teaching one class a week at the institute, on Wednesdays, and yet being revered as a treasure for her artistic sense of harmony, oneness, and focus on the next art form of her choosing, slowly transforming it into the next figure in her yard. Her six students would have the opportunity to take the ferry to her house in San Raphael, and enjoy a pleasant chat, while lying around, creating, thinking, being in the moment of artistic heaven.

The longer Celia reflected she thought of their trip to Wellfleet last year, and the first morning of her layering class, and how dreary and overcast the sky had been, and yet, the charm of watching Leroy navigate around the cape, its darkness gently hanging over the lake. It was all so mystical.

They enjoyed walking around Provincetown, stopping in shops, then flying back over to Boston to have dinner at an old, famous restaurant. She reminded him to get tickets for next month's ASO performance of Mahler's Songs of the Wayfarer (1885), Beethoven's Overture #3 to Lenore (1806), and Mahler's symphony #4 (1900), guest Mezzo-Soprano the world-renowned Teresa V. Borah. He said he would order them in the morning, soon after they arrived home.

CHAPTER TWO

Cynthia Tucker worked for Brewer Gas Company, a provider of natural gas to the metro area. As head of pipe maintenance, she made sure there were no leaks and performed her job well. She had a staff of 70 that monitored the flow of gas to their 2,000,000 customers. A Systems Structure degree from Georgia Tech had led her here 17 years ago, and while studying finance at Georgia State University she had met Jake Austin. He casually helped her research a method by which gas leaks could be discovered by sound wave variance, and once it was put into practice, patented, and sold to the state for 16.5 million dollars she had given Jake $800,000 dollars as a bonus. They formed a nice bond, however, their paths diverged over the next 15 years. Six years after receiving her master's she developed a schematic which routed nuisance calls back to the source, and authorities were able to discern, then ascertain the repeated off-color path using a simple kaleidoscope, and thus identify the troublemaker. It helped media and financial companies secure transactions by way of a loose-fitting encryption. She sold the technology for 2.3 billion dollars and entered the world of mergers, acquisitions, and downstream idea development with a four year close out. She contacted Jake when she heard about his astute handling of the sale of Triple Line Systems.

*

Jake and Marie sat at home resting from the travel. Jake would have to fill in tomorrow and teach a Sunday school class, and Marie would handle cashier duties in the kitchen as usual. The kids had asked to stay back to watch a certain TV documentary but would come to church later for the main service. Ashley had her driver's license now and they all were becoming more responsible in their actions and requests.

"Leroy and Celia are so good to be around," Marie observed.

"Yes, decent, fun, and smart."

"Do you ever think you could do it; I mean, did you ever consider dating across lines?"

"Not really, it never came my way, and we never talked about it as a family. How about you?" he asked his wife.

"We never talked about it either, it just never seemed an option, really. In my circle, it never came up. I guess we were kind of closed off," Marie says to Jake.

"How about for the kids? Is there something we need to say, or ask?" Jake poses.

"We probably do need to have some conversation, you know, basic preservation stuff," Marie mentions.

"Legacy, birthright?" he questions aloud.

"You know, I don't know where it fits, but the more I think, it seems important," Marie shares.

"Wow, I guess we do need to talk more about beliefs for the future. Regarding Celia and Leroy, I never even blinked, ever since I've known them, never thought about it?"

"Because they're older?" she asks.

"This is deep, wow. Let's think some more and revisit this," Jake offers.

"Let's. It's important. May have implications for your work?" she says to him.

"Yeah, a global view. Thanks babe."

"You, too."

They cuddle a bit and drift off to restful sleep.

CHAPTER THREE

"So, from a management perspective, how do we use this information to hire, and get a sense of a corporation's culture?"

"First off what I want to see is whether the Black guy gets a chance in another industry, consumer products, for example?" Susan Wheeler speaks up.

"What Black guy?" Jake Austin asks the student.

"Leon, just out of prison," she responds.

"Where did it identify him as black?"

Susan, like the other students, search their memories, then review the file. After a few seconds, Harvey Johnson speaks up.

"Assumptions, based on pre-conceived notions. If he went to prison, or just got out of prison, he must be black. All the good that he had done in a short period was discounted or filtered out."

"Susan?" Jake opens the conversation.

"Well, I must agree. Most of what I've seen or heard led me there as well," she admits.

"Have any of you actually met 'Leon'?" Jake asks.

The class shifts a bit in their seats, two hands go up.

"Mark," Jake gestures to another student.

"This is not a fair scenario. This is not the real world. Employers don't get this much information on people," he offers.

"No, but every business model says you should know this about people, and thus the argument for start-up company XX, and their L56 unit which follows potential hires for two weeks, records behavior, sends a report, then destroys the information gathered. You would have a fairly good idea about how someone is going to shape up," Jake presents.

"But is that fair, or legal?" Jamie Stevens speaks up.

"It's some of the data you must consider when making these deals," Jake says to them. "Look up at the screen," he then clicks on his slides. "Integrated risks models, relevant for 2016 and beyond? Compliance, growth and competitiveness, Basel III norms? And ultimately, the natural hierarchy and how that will be represented to develop and grow the business, based on the worker pool and what investors think about this kind of company? Okay, that's it for today. We'll discuss Maddie, a forty something widowed mom in the morning."

The group of twelve applaud and thank Mr. Austin for his stirring lecture.

*

Randall Brewer read in The Financial Character that Jake Austin now worked for H.U.N., and that Leroy Fleming was his lead man. Jake had proved his business acumen in the buyout of WES, and eventual sale of the merged companies, but Randall did not think he was at the level of skill necessary to play in the billionaire's club. Sure, he obviously learned a lot of moves from Wallace Henson, and he's applied whatever intellectual heritage he commands, but he should not be in this league, Randall kept thinking. "Maybe that's why he hired Leroy, something about the high and the low being closely related. Maybe Jake knows more about the Bruce Walker affair than I want to give him," Randall was thinking to himself. Of course, the bureau of prisons offered no specific information, even to Randall as Walker's attorney of record, so he knew he would have to consult some back sources to complete his aim of compromising Leroy, and maybe Jake Austin.

*

Dr. Joyce Taylor was feeling better about the whole saga of her journey with Bruce and WES. She was forty-five now and had a lot of good living ahead of her. She no longer felt the need to be in Colorado, and Toni was enjoying school, developing nicely as a first grader. She was proving to be a good single parent, and now wanted to use her professional credentials again towards some worthy endeavor. She still cherished those brief moments with Bruce, and even with the finances to do as she pleased there was still a curious emptiness, a longing for a close relationship with an equal partner, something Bruce Walker could never give her. She felt silly about moving to Florence, Colorado to be near him, knowing there would be no visitation with him at the super-max facility, or that he could comfort her in any other way. It was just he had made her feel whole, excited, and even needed by this man of dubious consequence. She didn't understand the totality of the experience but was resigned to the fact that she needed to go, and find a life, elsewhere.

*

The office Cynthia provided for Jake was large and impressive. The chairs were plush, with fine fabric, tables were mahogany and cherry wood, lamps, wall paintings, and such were very modern in design and structure. Jake's desk and chair sat near, facing a window, such that he would have to turn around when people entered. The ten feet high ceiling offered a sense of drama and moment peculiar to the well moneyed. None of these folks liked to feel cornered, or boxed into something, and even Jake's choice of desk position led clients who entered to feel in control.

Leroy's office, down the hall, was much smaller, though at 20'x 30', was adequate for the fine tuning he usually had to do when completing details of a deal or researching a project. Others could relax in there, and utilize the necessary digital equipment, and not feel less than the power brokers up the hall. Leroy didn't care one way or the other, he just wanted to get the job done and enjoy the ride. His only issue was that a Charles Rutherford had left messages on his office phone inquiring about Bruce Walker, and what happened to him. He couldn't tell if it was a threat or general inquiry of some kind, but he had let it slide until the tenth one was recorded, then he called the person back.

"Mr. Rutherford, this is Leroy Fleming, you have something for me?" Leroy asked.

"Thanks for calling back," the voice said. "We need to talk."

"Yes, about what?"

"My client wants to know how you killed Bruce Walker."

"Sure, of course, when do I meet them?" Leroy asked him.

Stunned by the response, Mr. Rutherford responded, "Soon. We'll call you back."

Leroy hung up the phone and activated the trace system which led to the law office of Mr. Randall Brewer. "Okay," Leroy said to himself, "he can't let it rest."

CHAPTER FOUR

Jake arrived at the office about 6:30a, walked in, then stepped back out. He had decided that he wanted to hit the streets today, view the passersby, get a sense of what another real world looked and felt like. He wasn't sure if he would just ride around or get out and walk a bit. A month ago, he bought an older, somewhat beat up vehicle from a buy here, pay here lot to use with clients who needed to be knocked down a peg, or rather, tested on a humility scale. So far, the three tested didn't flinch, and got in the car, and seemed to enjoy the ride out for lunch. Something about old and worn appealed to some of these younger, well-financed, risk takers. He phoned Leroy once he was out of the parking garage.

"Leroy, good morning."

"Hey boss, what's up?"

"I think I'm going to ride down in the hood to see what I can see," he shares.

"Research?" Leroy asks.

"I guess it could be, but more a sense of what it looks and feels like to be at the bus stop, or hang in front of a liquor store, or simply walk the streets and see who goes into the laundry mat, or just walk and see people come out of a corner store. So, I guess research in the sense of a better understanding, see what I feel and think," Jake gives him. "Anything new?"

"Just the usual call backs, though we do need to talk to the ladies with the silk screen partitions. They believe in a 300 million revenue post within four years. We at least need to have them come in," Leroy shares.

"I think so. Schedule, and have Cynthia attend as well."

"Okay, will do. See you later."

Jake hangs up and smiles as he starts out on his journey.

*

Cynthia had agreed to meet with Frank and Danny Oakley of Lifetime Focus Group, Ltd. out of Phoenix, Arizona. Their money came from the illegal marijuana trade back in Tennessee, then jumped huge in the legal trade, and now want to grow their gun sales and training salon business. They were expecting a $1.8 billion play moving operations overseas, but stock, employment, and distribution would be handled here in the U.S. The four-year build-out would net around six hundred thousand per year, and 2.5 hundred would be made by H.U.N. for its finances. All legal and business practice checks were positive, as nothing from the illegal days traced back to them, initially. Jake was given all the background information and would sit in on the approval stage of negotiations. He had given Leroy the package to look over and Leroy sent back a text, 'Bruce Walker-Tennessee Murders, 2011.' Jake paused, deleted the text, and thought whether to share this with Cynthia privately, or wait for the appropriate moment in the discussion with the Oakley brothers, and see how they react. If he told her beforehand, she might refuse to see them and lose a chance to gain some information about a growing trend in hidden money sources. Also, he didn't want her tainted by the kind of knowledge Leroy really brought in his capacity as Jake's assistant. Either way it would be a growth experience.

"Frank, Danny, come in and have a seat. This is Jake Austin, our executive vice president for investments," she gestures all around, and the two men stop short of sitting to shake Jake's hand. "Actually, have you all met before?" she asks.

"No, but we know of his work," Danny speaks up. "We used some of Henson Technologies' wafers in our communications towers back in 2011. We were a part of Tangy Tech out of Alaska before they bought Triple Line."

"Oh yeah, I remember," Jake responds.

"Okay, good," Cynthia steps in. "Frank, anything else we should know about international tariffs?"

"Our legal department has spent hours with the trade commission, and they said we were cleared for 200 shops on the designated four continents. No issues with our partners," Frank, the younger brother reports.

"Danny, again, why us?" Cynthia asks.

"Your integrity, financial resources, and everyone we approached brought up your name," Danny offers.

"Jake, any reason we should not put up the money?" Ms. Tucker asks, looking over to Jake, then to Danny and Frank.

Jake pauses, stands, and walks over closer to his boss. "I do have a question about Bruce Walker."

You could almost hear the knife go into the two bodies, and Cynthia's loss of oxygen. She starts to question Jake, but sat still, powerless over what would happen next. The two Oakley boys stood, and without a word, walked out of the conference room. After a few seconds, Jake hands her a copy of the indictment papers, and Bruce's conviction of the six murders. "Weed money," Cynthia verbalizes.

"Yes," Jake replies. "There's a lot of it around. This was a good test case."

"Jake, should I ask you how you were able to go there?" she asks him.

"Superb background research by my assistant, Mr. Fleming," Jake gives her.

"Well thank him for me," she responds.

"I will, he'd appreciate hearing that."

"Okay, next case."

*

Driving back near Fisherman's Warf Danny and Frank Oakley talked about the day Bruce Walker killed those seven men. Only six bodies were found hanging from the trees because Bruce had burned one body to a crisp and mixed the remains in with some dead animals further back into the woods. They remembered the crazed expression on his face, after his men took their weapons, and how he screamed and hollered at them for trying to take his weed and destroy his enterprise. It was a good deal spoiled by bad actors who were playing in the wrong league. They should have stuck to rolling 'pounders' back in the city. How they got put on to this level of trade was never clear, and not many questions were asked, or answers given, by anyone who was present that day.

The Oakley's trailer was early, and they loaded their eight tons quickly, paid the fare, and had their driver leave Clifftop, Tennessee, and drive west out I-40. He would be contacted later about the exact destination of the load. Bruce's men had hurried about, on the small runway, emptying the plane, stuffing greenbacks into large containers, and using hand trucks to set them up in the plane's storage compartment, where two men grabbed them, positioned them, and made room for the next one. $98.4 million dollars were already bundled, and when the Chicago people arrived and paid, the total would go to 120.2 million. Well, that was what was supposed to happen, but those clowns had come to rob the outdoor marketplace but were proficiently subdued by the well-trained security personnel. When Bruce came out of the shed, he decided to send a message, and thus the hanging. Each conspirator saw a buddy hang until the last one, who had to witness the burning, before his own demise. It was ugly, and the Oakley brothers were glad they practiced 'safe sex,' as it were, and met no harm when dealing with Mr. Walker's gang of thugs. It was the last time they bought marijuana through those back channels. At trial, they were given immunity, and disguised, and only had to answer yes three times, and Bruce Walker was convicted and given the death penalty. That event from thirteen years ago was just a bad memory, until this afternoon. Hopefully, being turned down on this deal would be the only consequence left for them, from that era.

CHAPTER FIVE

"Mr. Foster, we think it's time for you to retire," said the voice on the other end of the transmission.

"When does it start?" Leonard Foster asked his supervisor.

"Immediately."

Leonard looked at the work phone on his desk and could hear it power off. Next, the PC screen before him went dark, and shut down.

"What should I do with the devices?" he asked.

"A courier will be there in an hour to collect them from you," David Settles informed him. "HR will e-mail the particulars of your settlement. Thank you for your good work."

"Yes, thank you David."

Leonard hung up his land line system, shredded two documents he had just copied, and took his latest read from the bookshelf. He read for an hour, called Susie, informed her of the change, then slept for two hours. It was 4:30pm when he woke up, and the news flash on TV caught his attention, "Arthur Davis, Billionaire Investor, head of SixFive Global Industries jumped to his death from a 17th floor apartment on Dexter Avenue. He was recently indicted on federal corruption charges and had suffered financial losses of at least 2.3 billion dollars. His wife Delores, 62, was recently diagnosed with brain cancer, and given two months to live. He was 61.

"Damn," Leonard exclaimed, scaring the two cats resting near him, one on the couch, the other crouched on the floor. They looked at him briefly, then looked away, having no answers for him. Leonard thought he would go for a short walk in the woods, smoke a joint, and let it all settle in, before he made any moves. Susie would get home about six and they could talk then. Mr. Settles, standing at the window, watching a plane taxi out, had two calls to make before boarding his plane to Wisconsin. His assistant, Deborah Turner, had secured the servers and destroyed most of the incriminating evidence of deception. She didn't realize that Mr. Foster had put a file in place that contained all transactions from the past year. They too could be indicted soon.

*

The air was crisp, and the tree limbs were without leaves. Leonard walked and looked around at the fallen trees. He thought of their years living here, and how he would hate to move, though the real estate market was active, and they could make a handsome profit. It was near Susie's work, and the places they routinely visited so an adjustment would have to be made wherever they landed. His old friend Joe, and his wife Helen, had just moved in around the corner and it would be awkward to leave the area now, although they would understand. It would primarily be Susie's call because Leonard could work from anywhere, and there are many great neighborhoods within a twenty -mile radius, whether they wished to stay in town, or go outside the perimeter highway. Her preference had been to move to their vacation home on the island, but she had backtracked from that saying she was not ready to retire, though several companies out there would hire her in an instant. Leonard preferred the city and would state his case. Whatever their decision, if the time were right, they would know.

*

"Hey Deborah, David. How's it going?"

"Just fine except one little problem, I noticed a runner had been attached to server 16," she reported.

"What does that mean?" he asked.

"Someone made a file."

"What do you mean a file?"

"Someone recorded transactions."

"Leonard?"

"I can't say. Maybe Arthur had it done?" she speculated.

"Which would be worse?" he asked.

"Equal."

"How?"

"Leonard is a stoner and could do something dumb. Arthur may have given it to someone. When are you coming back?"

"Tuesday."

"Okay."

They both sit in place for a moment, David in his office at the farm, Deborah in her study at home, nursing a glass of wine. David was angry at himself for not overseeing file dissipation more carefully, and Deborah was planning how much she would share with the feds if she were called in. Both wished they had not met each other.

*

Arthur Davis was born poor and smart. He was hustling comic books and favors by the age of 12. In high school, he sold a little pot, ventured into stolen appliances, and got into day trading after graduation. He not only had a knack for picking winners but understood margins. He thought in terms of weekly salaries, and in three years was running the investment arm of CAT Care Holdings, a financial firm that sold investments to short-term investors. It was close to a Ponzi type scheme, but Arthur never dipped into the funds of others. He kept accounts separate and made good money for himself and his customers. His main challenge was from drug dealers he knew from high school who wanted to clean up their profits, but again, he stayed free of compromising situations. People who had one to two thousand dollars to invest for a year became his primary clients. After 18 months, they could collect what was earned or sign up for another term. By 1986 he had a roster of 1,600 clients and a fund of $69 million dollars.

He met Delores Baker at the Tot's Toys fund drive put on by Weathersby Hospital each year. They were $60,000.00 short of their goal as of Christmas Eve 1987, and he hand delivered a check for that amount from his personal account. The attraction was mutual and instant, and they began dating and were married a year later. It was the first for both. She continued her career as a nurse, and head of the yearly fundraiser. Arthur's business continued an upward climb, and they enjoyed a prosperous and engaged lifestyle. Interestingly, neither wanted kids, and it was never discussed.

CHAPTER SIX

Larry Fleming was beginning to feel as if he were back at work. Even though he had been able to keep office hours to Tuesdays and Thursdays he was averaging four sessions a day. He finally admitted to himself that he was enjoying the work again, and if this is what semi-retirement looks like he'll take it. Sixty-three was feeling good these days.

"Larry Fleming, may I help you?" he answered the first call of the day.

"Yes sir. My name is Leonard Foster, and I was given your name by a friend. She thinks I have some issues with marijuana that need to be explored, and you come highly recommended," he shares.

"Well, I am a counselor. When would you like to come in," Larry asks him?

"Next week maybe," he answers.

"I have an opening this Thursday at 11 o'clock," Larry responds.

"Thank you very much. I'll see you then."

"Okay. Have a good day."

*

Larry started thinking about people in their sixties who smoke marijuana. He had a few friends who smoke occasionally, and three clients presently who have been dependent on the weed for a long time. One was a factory worker who built cars for thirty-three years. He was a Vietnam veteran, married for 35 years, he and his wife raised three kids, paid off the house, and have a nice retirement going at 66 years of age. He still makes a few dollars on the side helping folks with different chores, and she does taxes each year for about 20 people they've known for years. She smokes a couple of times a week to relax, but he smokes every day. Basically, he's a zombie, and has been on auto pilot for the past twenty years, bowling each Tuesday with the same team, washing both cars every Sunday morning when the weather is nice, minds the grandkids, when necessary, but generally is holed up in his den watching television most of the time. For them it's a comfortable lifestyle with limited involvement in the affairs of others. They take about four good trips a year, three on the road, and the other by plane, usually out west somewhere. The weed connection is usually made beforehand, and they bliss out wherever they go, seeing just enough sites, or attending just enough events to make the trip worthwhile. Their health is good, and their foggy, near melancholy life is satisfying. Their sessions are about having a safe place to talk and iron out any miscommunications the past month. They've been coming to see Larry for about a year now.

The other one, female, just turned 60, has been on marijuana maintenance for the past ten years. She finally kicked the heroin habit, but won't, and probably can't leave the weed alone after all these years. She's the classic wine with dinner, twice divorced, executive secretary who has two cats, and the on-again, off-again relationship with the plumber down the street. He's a year younger and comes by a couple times a month for a movie, sex, and sometimes will smoke with her. It works for both, and they kind of stay out of the way, are responsible, and are generally happy with the arrangement. His marriage has been one of convenient cover for his wife's other interests. She and her friend travel a lot.

*

His next call was from Leroy who sounded anxious.

"Hey broh, what's up?" spoke Larry recognizing his brother's voice.

"You know, you got a minute?" Leroy asks him.

"Got two for you; tell it."

"You know, I may need to speak to you outdoors on this one," Leroy thinks aloud.

"Whatever."

"Look, I'm in San Fran right now, and I'll be in Atlanta next week. What day is good for you?" Leroy asks him.

"Wednesday, all day."

"Okay, I'll call you when I get in town; about noon maybe?"

"Sounds great to me."

"Okay, all right. Thanks."

"All right brother, take care."

"Okay, see you then."

*

The security officer motioned for the limousine driver to move the vehicle from the reserved area until he recognized Senator Cyrus Walker in the back seat. He then stepped to the door, opened it, and helped the senator, ninety-seven years old from his seat.

"Thank you, young man," he said as he shook the officer's hand and moved past him. Cyrus walked into the building, straight up, went to the elevator and pushed the call button. When the elevator door opened several older lawyers, going out for lunch, spoke to the old man, and hurried off. Cyrus got into the car alone, pushed for the 8th floor, and rested on his cane, gently. Randall was waiting when he reached the floor.

"Randall, my boy, how are you?" spoke the powerful man.

"Mr. Walker, I'm fine. Come right on in," Randall gestured, and allowed the man to walk past him, going to his office.

"Where would you like for me to sit?" the old man asked as Randall closed the door and went to his chair behind the desk.

"How about your favorite chair, the love seat?" Randall offered, knowing full well that's the chair he always chose.

"Thank you, son, yes, I'll sit here."

Cyrus took his seat, sat straight up, looked around the room and stretched his long legs and arms, as if to test distances to the walls. His cane was knocked to the floor, and neither man moved to retrieve it. Cyrus looked at Randall, who looked at him, and then they moved on.

"Randall, your daddy was a good man, and he helped my nephew out a lot. Bruce could be a hand full, but your pa knew how to handle him. You know our families go back to the eighteen twenties, and everybody made a lot of money on the slave trades, then on to banking and the law. You've done well, and that boy Bruce, well, I don't think we know how much money he made. But you might. When he was younger, and worked for the DEA, he made some great busts and made some terrible mistakes. He and that colored boy, Leroy, had some problems, but somehow, they stayed friends. I need you to find out who killed Bruce, and how they did it?"

Cyrus then stumbled over a few words, closed his eyes, and took a nap for twenty-five minutes. Randall sat in place and made some notes. When Cyrus awoke, Randall said, "Yes sir."

After their meeting, Randall Brewer informed Mr. Rutherford that his services were no longer needed. He was given a $10,000.00 severance and told not to come this way again. One other investigator, and his assistant of 5 years, Gail Greely, were let go as well. They both were given envelopes with a $15,000.00 check inside, after they signed a knowledge waiver which held them immune from testifying about legal matters addressed in the employ of Mr. Brewer. It wasn't really a binding agreement, by law, but both understood the implication. If they had not signed anything, they didn't know anything.

CHAPTER SEVEN

Even in maximum security Bruce Walker was feared. He had no ideology. He was a murderer, a technology wizard, a liar, and had connections everywhere. No one in the system believed his death was an accident, but the parlor game was not so much who, but how was it done? If he had been a religious zealot, that would have been one thing, evil genius, another. Just an angry man, well, not close? Drug dealer, poof? Something was just quite different about Mr. Walker, and no one could quite grasp the size of his criminal mind.

Few knew about Dr. Taylor, and the child, Toni. And fewer still knew that he really cared for them. Even Mary, his ex-wife, only rarely got the deep-down affection he was capable of giving. Only Dr. Joyce Taylor did something to his humanity that most felt was impossible. She gave him joy, and a true sense of pleasure. In one night, their affair allowed him to experience the joy usually reserved for a lifetime of good works. His having Randall Brewer write that check to her for $30 million was a reparation, paying a price for a service another has freely given. Unfortunately, he would never understand how a gift of generosity can alter one's behavior for the better. He was not able to sustain the change or continue a relationship of this nature.

*

Arthur Davis was introduced to factoring by David Settles. David was with a financial group that had made sizable profits picking up receivables from construction firms short on cash. Oddly, they met at a Video Gaming conference that Arthur backed financially, and where David sold 'runners.' Arthur showed some interest in the technology but thought there were more efficient ways to track transactions that were meant to be disguised. Anyway, Arthur researched the financial arrangement process and bought the company David worked for, keeping him on as vice-president. Within three years SixFive Global Industries had a portfolio valued at 3.4 billion dollars, half of which was in the form of monthly paybacks, by way of invoice discounting, a fourth was collateralized by physical assets, and the rest was money in the bank. The exposure was evenly split between home and international accounts, and was all very discreet, and satisfying. Arthur was a happy man.

Trouble came about, however, when Delores was diagnosed with inoperable brain cancer, and he tried to bribe the FDA to expedite approval of a drug that had shown promise in 75% of the testing. They had reported that it would take another six months to be conclusive, but she was only given four months to live using current therapies. Arthur started spreading money around using his cousin, Joe Rubin, to act as his conduit to decision makers within the trial department. Joe was a lobbyist and was well known in the health care industry. He knew who to approach, and who would see him.

What Arthur remembered, at the awards dinner a year ago, for counselors who worked with incarcerated veterans, Delores was so elegant looking, and poised, yet, had a faraway look that said something was wrong. They had a doctor's appointment the following week, and his suspicion was verified, brain tumor, 8mm, near the frontal lobe, imbedded in tissue such that surgery would risk rupture. They would have to try chemo, instead of radiation. Everything was just all wrong, and so unfortunate for this wonderful lady. There was a sense of urgency, and Arthur conveyed that to Joe.

*

"Your memory is divorced from the experience, yet people know when they meet you whether you were a cop or a counselor, adventurous or straight, handy or dependent, and so it goes," Larry was telling Leonard before he left the session. "There are a lot of secrets there, and you may never know them."

Leonard drove off from the counseling session somewhat panicked as he wasn't sure what all he'd done at SixFive the last few years. His so-called retirement was rather abrupt, and no reasons had been given. He had a strange feeling that David and Deborah were up to something, and perhaps he was part of some kind of espionage, but what, he could not recall, or maybe it was something from a TV series he'd seen, he was the bad guy, or the good guy, he just couldn't remember.

Deborah Lorraine Turner, graduated with distinction, played tennis, and didn't necessarily like men. Her father was kind and supportive, but slapped her once when she was a teen, and she had never forgiven him. She figured most men would do that at some point in a relationship, so she rarely allowed men to get close to her. She craved success and money and went after it when she graduated and moved to Atlanta in 1995. She tried marketing and banking, then retrained as a computer analyst in 2004, and met David who needed someone with varied experience to record and analyze data for a company he had joined. She hired on, was approved by Arthur Davis, and quickly showed skill in creative economic thinking. She understood left and right-side movements, and the effects on investments, payouts, and credit structure if not handled properly. She knew what drag default amounts had on revenues of a hundred million before she wrote the algorithm. She helped David better understand the risks of factoring, and placement of 'sure' bets. She would get to know staff as part of due diligence, and not just have phone calls with administrative people. She trusted data but trusted the actions of people to determine their credit worthiness more accurately. A drunk CEO, with sterling credit, would ultimately become a risk. Not all money was good money.

*

"What do we do about Leonard?" Deborah asked David when they met to plan the press release. The company's legal firm would handle the funeral, and care for Delores her final days, but they had to be ready for possible government action. Neither wanted to go through a long, legal process, and they certainly didn't want to go to jail. She informed him that she had found the 'runner' that was used to record the transactions, but now they had to prove it was Leonard, and what he planned to do with the information he had, and more importantly, what did he have? Financial favors to corporate friends are one thing, but bribery is another. Arthur really should not have done that, but he loved his wife and wanted her cured! They hoped it was nothing more.

CHAPTER EIGHT

"How did it go with the doctor?" Susie asked her husband when he arrived back home.

"He's not a doctor. He's not even a therapist. He's just a counselor," Leonard reported, somewhat angrily.

"A counselor! Wow, was he helpful?"

"He's pretty good," Leonard states as he settles into his favorite chair, a lounger with thick padding.

"Are you going back to see him?" she asks.

"I think so, he's pretty interesting."

"Well good, maybe you'll make a friend."

They both laugh.

"You know, I probably could use a friend, right now," Leonard offers. "I see him again next week."

"Good, he probably could use the work," she says, putting him on.

"He's a Black guy you know?"

"Does that matter to you?"

"Not really. I felt like I was talking to a peer."

"That's encouraging."

"He's pretty sharp, he's been there, and done that, and not just the drugs. Some things he said he couldn't talk about, from his days in the military."

"Now who was there for counseling?"

"No, he just mentioned that in passing to help me relax. I think he knows I have a lot of secrets myself."

"He could tell that in one hour?"

"An hour and a half really. I think he's that good, whatever his certifications say, I think he knows his stuff."

"If you say so. How much today?"

"Four hundred."

"And each session?"

"One fifty."

"Well, okay. Do your thing. How long does he think you should come see him?"

"He says at least a year, at least that's about what it takes for people my age who've been smoking since the hippie days. He says we've been living, and doing, but unconscious, nevertheless. The ones of us who have survived are damaged beyond note, and in ways that require thorough investigation."

"I'm not saying a word."

"Good, because I'm about to destroy my stash. Do you want any of it?"

"Yeah, leave me enough for a few joints."

"All right darling, I will. Are we going to the movies with Joe and Helen this weekend?"

"I think so. I'll call Helen tomorrow and confirm."

"Okay, thanks. What's for dinner?"

"I don't know, let's go out?"

"Let's do it. Our favorite new place?"

"Yes, that would be good."

"Okay."

*

Leroy was feeling sick again. He felt overburdened by his past life, even though years of good had balanced the equation. He was judging the behavior of others, usually mild irritants now felt like major disappointment. It was in his chest. Mentally, he couldn't put together what a criminal he had been, and that all his 'friends' had been sociopaths, and that even though he has done well the past eighteen years he would have to look at himself the way society would judge him, if only they knew the details. Something about the Oakley boys and their relationship to Bruce Walker set him off, and he felt lousy again, as if crooks were all around, and maybe that he should not be working for Jake at all, that somehow his past could taint the good work he would do. Yet, Jake needed him, and Cynthia needed Jake, and what Leroy brought to the table was more valuable than he realized. Not only was this serious money they played with, but these were serious people who could do tremendous good for the world when given the capital, and proper restraints to create the next generation of human intelligence formation as humanity was on the verge of another leap in understanding why humans act the way they do. Robots were nice, but it's all about human growth. Leroy had to view his present disturbance not so much as an aberration, but a necessary piece of emotional growth. He was getting better prepared, not falling apart.

*

Larry Fleming's oldest friend was dying. He had requested one visitor, and the arrangements were set in place by the Bureau of Prisons in Washington. Herbert Junior had been in maximum lockdown the past twenty years, eight in Marion, and twelve in Florence and the medical tests said he had about a month to live. Herbert wanted to have one last conversation with the one person on planet earth that understood his pain.

The visiting room was pristine, and the warden agreed to the terms that the two men would be left in a room with a window and no guards. Their thirty-minute conversation would not be recorded, at least by them. Larry arrived at precisely eight-fifteen a.m. and was promptly taken to the room upstairs. Herbert looked old and weak and could not stand to greet his friend. They did not shake hands. After Larry sat down, they looked at each other for a moment and Herbert went into a nod that reminded Larry of the heroin days. They sat like that for about a minute, and Herbert opened his eyes, and smiled at his friend.

"When did you get here?" Herbert asked him.

"An hour ago, they had to search and interview me," Larry told him.

"Good, I told them you might be packing," Herbert said, making a joke.

"I should have, back then," Larry says to him, and they both laugh.

"I loved her you know, but her brother and those stupid clowns just couldn't let it go," Herbert says, cryptically. "Thank you for what you did in Germany. That had to be tough, but necessary. You and the military?"

"Even."

"Good. Tell Leroy his case is closed, 'The Case for Larry Fleming' however, is ongoing!" Herbert starts to laugh, and Larry joins him.

Herbert then nods off again, and Larry sits with his friend for ten more minutes, then the guards let him out. Herbert died an hour later.

*

Jake was disheartened by what he was seeing. He felt a sense of pity that was new to him. Seeing the downtrodden this close, smelling the stench of stale alcohol and body fluids on the homeless alcoholics, being in the presence of women so thin, scarred, and lifeless was almost too painful to bare. He stood for ten more minutes, in front of, then to the back of the liquor store, watching the ones who had a few coins dig into their pockets, retrieve the amount, and toss it ever so gently into the cupped hand of Simon, waiting for offers from anyone near to add to the pot so that another communal bottle could be bought. Jake added 75 cents, getting a smile from the 'banker' and the other men as this amount achieved the first goal. When the fifth size bottle was brought out, and opened, gulps were taken and the bottle was passed, quickly to whomever was standing near, whether they had donated to the cause, or not. Jake politely refused, thinking of the possible germs shared, and moreover that this was not that kind of research, he did not need to try and fit in, he was an interested observer, not so much to help these folks himself, but to view, up close, a social practice that brought people together, not so much in shared suffering, but a communal ritual of deep significance. Jake would not pretend to know what this was like every day, two, three times a day. He could not understand this pain, of this type, practices entered slowly, violently at times, for whatever reason, shared, known, accepted perhaps, due to the bottom rung of life experience, here, where there would be no out for most, only a few, by the grace of God, and perhaps by something Jake would learn here today and express in a business model. He wasn't sure. This was desperation beyond money, or witness, this was old, historical.

*

"David, I've found out what he knows, or rather, what he's done!" Deborah almost shouted into the phone. "And I think I know about the 'runner.' It's like a traffic cop, new on the job, dressed like the regular guy, but he sends one car the wrong way, on purpose. Arthur transferred two million dollars of company money to Leonard for 'information.' The kicker is that there was a note that four more was supposed to be sent to him, but went to another account, to a Mr. Rubin, yet again for 'information,'" she shared with him.

"How long ago?" he asked her.

"Six months ago, about the time Delores was first diagnosed."

"Do you think there's a connection?" he asked.

"I don't know, I'm just saying," she offered.

"Two million to Leonard, and four to this Mr. Rubin? Do you know him?" David asks her.

"I don't know. Two people come to mind, but I'm not sure why Arthur, wait a minute, the health care thing," she offers, somewhat muddily.

"You mean the medicine?"

"Yes, FDA approval. I bet he's the guy Arthur had bribe the doctor, the head of the trial."

"If this is true, this is not good. We're a part of that whole stream of transactions," David surmises.

"So, it's possible Leonard may know about our 'business'?" she responds.

"Yes. Do you think Delores knows about Arthur's death?" David presents to her.

"I doubt it. She went into a coma two weeks before he jumped, and I don't think she has that much longer to live," Deborah responds. "Are you responsible for any administration of the estate?" she further asks him.

"No. Actually, Arthur was in discussions with H.U.N., Ltd., to sale, or merge his research firm, Wind Chase. It's been in operation for 15 years. It's in China. I only had a brief conversation with him about it," he tells her.

"Why didn't I know about that?" she questions him.

"Executive privilege. Arthur's company, his rules," David gives her.

They both sat quietly, listening to the beat of schemes gone awry. Partners in one sense, but potential enemies in another.

"So, what about us?" Deborah breaks the silence.

"I don't know. Our plans are on hold, that's for sure. I don't know. We should be getting a letter from Cynthia Turner, the head of H.U.N. soon. I don't think we should say anything more about anything, except corporate matters in our area of expertise."

"You mean?"

"Nothing."

CHAPTER NINE

Delores was a good nurse. She knew when to coddle, and when to be stern. Her family was blessed with good genes and good health and were an attractive lot. She left home at twenty, started nursing school and roomed with three other young women for two years, in a nice apartment not far from the campus. After graduation, she took a job in a doctor's office for a year, got some more training and heard about a job in a psychiatric hospital. She worked the detox unit for a time, then moved to the dual diagnosis unit and became the medication nurse on the evening shift, earning shift differential pay. She dated Eric, a med surge doc for a few years, but he took a job in another state, and she did not want to leave Georgia. They continued to talk a bit, but the attraction was not strong enough for them to try long distance dating. After a few months, their infrequent calls to each other stopped.

She blossomed in her work, becoming shift supervisor, and eventually day charge nurse. As her administrative duties increased, she took on the lead for the hospital's charity work, handling fund raisers and the outreach programs. She achieved high praise and honors and met Arthur when he donated a large sum to complete a financial goal. The attraction was instant, and they married in about year, and have enjoyed a good life together. She followed some of his business dealings but stayed busy with her work and maintaining their comfortable homes in town and on the island. They travelled well and had a good circle of friends.

*

Arthur could be mean and biting in some of comments. He was particular about how things should be done and followed through. He was generally kind and supportive and people who worked for him were loyal. He had been able to build successful companies with minimal staff. He hired well, paid well, and gave people a chance to start over if there had been some disturbance in their past. His core management team of three were all bright and strait laced, with two of them joining SixFive Global within weeks of graduating college. One was the daughter of a valued friend. The other six employees were good, hard-working specialists who performed well. The average length of service was twelve years. David and Deborah came on about the same time and were good managers. They were in their early thirties and had enough experience to fashion how things worked in financial matters. Arthur was routinely surprised by some of the products they would present, not all adopted, but some solid winners. It was the factoring business, introduced by David, which kicked the company into overdrive, and the billionaire's club. Things went very well until David and Deborah got greedy, and Arthur fudged on some values based on his wife's illness.

*

Joseph Phillip Rubin was just an old-fashioned player. He bent rules, told lies, and laughed a lot. A lot of people loved him, or rather used him to carry out the back-door stuff that needed to be done, always for the right reasons. He served two years in federal prison for bank fraud and had just completed three years of supervised release when Arthur talked to him. They met in Arizona, near the Grand Canyon in the fall of 2014.

Joe was tall and lanky, and had that smile that said, "I'm your friend!" He was a great conversationalist, left leaning, but with no political participation. He believed in justice for all but would not go out of his way to help the downtrodden. In prison, he was a loner but was connected to the right people and had no worries. He always had money for commissary, clean clothes, and good books to read. He stayed away from the drugs, and the gambling crowd.

The air and sky were clear, and a cool breeze was about. Arthur had left the hotel to go up the long stretch of road to a local eatery for breakfast. It was about a mile's walk, and he enjoyed the time to freshen his thinking about what he was about to discuss. At 5'10" 180 lbs. he was athletic and sure of purpose in his presentation, and people sensed that the closer they got to him. He didn't like long conversations, but would explore the subtleties of what was said, if not clear. He had made good money staying on the edge of propriety as most of the businesspeople he knew were used to cutting corners, and usually knew where they were, and how not to get cut. He knew this was risky, but he loved his wife, and wanted her illness cured. Joe had driven up and was seated in a booth when Arthur arrived. They recognized each other by use of a pre-arranged hand gesture.

"Joe, how are you?" Arthur spoke as he joined the man.

"I'm fine, it's been a while," Joe spoke.

"Have you ordered?" Arthur asked, looking around, his discomfort showing as he looked around to see who was doing what in the place.

"Just coffee," said Joe as he looked at the menu before him. "Standard fare looks like. The guy from the hotel said it should be adequate."

"I can do adequate," spoke Arthur as he pulled a small menu from between the glass salt and pepper shakers sitting in the middle of the four-seater table.

It was a modest sized restaurant area, with about seven customers present. It was coded for 65. Both men looked around and surmised that they could talk freely without too much intrigue. Low tones would suffice.

"Are you seeking global, quick time approval, or single client approval?" Joe asked him.

"Global would look better, but I'm only concerned about my wife right now," Arthur answered.

"So, individual meds and administration?"

"If that can be arranged."

"You've tried other countries?"

"Yes, inferior products."

"Payments?"

"Through you. I already know the names."

"Cash a problem?"

"No. Whenever you're ready to leave I have the first installment."

"Good. Let's eat."

Joe left Arizona with $100,000.00 cash in a leather satchel and a check for $1.4 million in his wallet. He would see people next week and hand them bundles of cash, equal to their level of service. The three government officials would not be glad to see him, however, especially Dr. Monroe, but would take the cash, nevertheless.

*

Jake walked from the liquor store and turned onto MLK, Jr. Drive. He walked past several residences and was surprised how run down they were. He accepted these were people's homes, or if renters, it was where they lived. He did not feel secure here, as this was not his world. A young woman, thin and faceless, discounted from years of mental, physical, and spiritual abuse, approached him, and winked, and asked, "What do you need?"

Jake, startled, waves her off and sees the man walk up from his right. "What's up dude?" he asks, not getting too close, and reaching into his front, pants pocket. He motions the woman to back up. She does, and Jake thought of Leroy and something he told him once, "Talk shit, and go with the flow."

"Where's Grover?" Jake asked the man.

"He ain't 'round no more; what ya need?" the man asked again.

"I might need two but let me go get some money from my car," Jake replies.

"All right, I'll be here," the man said, figuring he had a sale.

Two other guys walk up to the man who makes an exchange of product for money and turns to watch Jake walk away. The woman rocks her head several times, and licks her lips, then goes behind the house. The man folds the cash up in his hand and follows her.

*

Leonard had not smoked any pot since his first session with Mr. Fleming. He felt strange and looked forward to talking to the counselor about it.

"Good morning Mr. Foster, come on in," Larry greeted him. "How are you today?"

"Good, but weird," Leonard says, sitting in the same chair he chose last week.

"What's weird?" Larry asks, not sitting behind his desk, having pulled his chair around to the side of it earlier.

Leonard pauses a moment, then responds.

"I'm bumping into things at home, and I don't have quick answers to questions like normal. Also, I'm sleeping more than usual, but I'm not having any cravings."

"You're becoming less high, and your body is adapting to the change. It's a long, slow healing process," Larry gives him.

"How long?"

"It's going to be a different kind of year for you if you stay clean," Larry mentions.

"A year!" Leonard questions.

"Yes. Mental, physical, spiritual change. In about a month you'll notice you're not high," Larry reports to him.

"You mean I'm high now?" Leonard further quizzes.

"Yep."

"This is trippy. How do you know?"

"Blood tests that show the level of THC in your system. We can get a quantitative from your urine as well. The levels drop slowly over time. Plus, behavioral changes. People will notice that you're acting differently before you do. In time, you'll have greater awareness about the environment, things you haven't noticed, or thought about in years will become important. You'll have more energy," Larry gives him.

"I'm not a dope fiend or a drunk you know?" Leonard states.

Larry lets a gentle laugh slip out.

"What's funny?" Leonard asks.

"Think for a minute," Larry says to him. "You've been smoking pot how long?"

"Okay, but I've never just stopped before," Leonard says. "You're right, I've had a buzz for a long time."

"You're going to be okay if you stick with it this time, I mean, total abstinence," Larry offers to him.

"No booze either?" he asks.

"Nothing. Do you have any health issues; are you on any medication?" Larry asks.

"No, good there. No cigarettes, no crack on the weekends," he shares to be funny.

"When was the last time you had a checkup, a complete physical?" Larry asks.

"It's been years," Leonard shares.

"Okay. I've got this assessment form I need you to fill out and bring back next week. It's pretty straight forward," Larry tells him. "We'll go over the answers and develop a treatment plan to help steer you through the bio/psych/social aspects of this deal. You'll be fine. Quickly, any legal or marital issues pressing at this time?"

"No. I'm pretty lame," he says.

"Good, we'll take it a step at a time, okay?"

"Okay boss. See you next week."

"Okay, have a good one."

Larry was glad the gentleman had come back.

CHAPTER TEN

When Jake returned to the office there was a detailed report from Leroy on his desk. The first page read:

SixFive Global Industries: Summary

1. Cash rich, experienced leader in Mr. Arthur Davis, experienced staff, but small, some past success in takeovers, but not at this level of complexity, would be time-consuming.
2. Problems!!
3. Cynthia has a copy.

*

Cynthia favored the deal and questioned Leroy's analytics. She felt his view was narrow and shared that with Jake in their morning meeting.

"This could be a top dog for us," she opened to Jake. "especially with their moves into health care."

"But Chase Winds has two drugs in trial that don't look as promising as they did a year ago, Arthur has exposure there," Jake offered.

"They only need one hit now that the purchase of the Delaney Group has gone forward. They have an outstanding array of drugs geared to the ageing population, plus, an exciting robotics division," she returns.

"Clinical Trials pg.2, Patent issues, page 12."

Cynthia flips to the pages and reads the passages.

"How did I miss those?" she questions herself. "Okay, I see. That could be a couple of years of litigation. We don't need that. Should we see the gentleman anyway?"

"I'm not sure it would be worth it. There could be some ethics violations because of what we know," Jake shares.

"What do we know?"

"Arthur may have a personal issue that could cloud his judgement."

"How so?"

"His wife is ill and could possibly benefit from one of the drugs under investigation."

"What are you suggesting?"

"Could be time sensitive."

"Can't we broker the deal and make our fee?"

"It may not be clean money."

"Let's have him in anyway. There's something to learn here."

"Sure. I'll set it up."

*

Celia had completed her winter painting course for the gifted, and again was excited by the production and creativity of the young folks. This year had meaning because her 60th birthday is next month, and the reach from there to here was so pronounced by the vision of her students. Not only because of electronic devices, but the representational skills for this period being so exotic and fresh. She felt she was given a special gift this year. Leroy had returned from his work out west, and they were having a meal of salmon, potatoes, and collards. She was having a glass of wine.

"Do you want to have a party for your birthday?" he asked her.

"I thought you'd never ask," she replies.

"Here, or on the island?"

"Here, I think, and on the island," she says.

They have a good laugh with that response.

"I think that's perfect. That way no one has to drive up and down the roads or fly in, get a room and all that, unless they want to attend them both. Sixty, that's rather good," Leroy offers.

"Yeah, I like this age, there's a certain freedom to it," she comments. "How was San Francisco?"

"Cold, but we got a lot done. Thanks again for your tip on healthcare, I would not have researched that, and something may have slipped by on a proposal we were considering," Leroy says to her.

"Now tell me again, what kind of money are we talking about?" she asks.

"I know, it's wild, but Jake seems to be comfortable. They throw two, three billion-dollar discussions around like its thousands. I'm glad I just do the research, and they make the decisions."

"So, what do you think of your boss, Ms. Tucker?" Celia asks him.

"She's intense, but successful. I think she's still trying to figure me out, and why Jake and I work so well together. I think he had to tell her that we are independent as well, though not at their level," Leroy shares.

"Well, that's good," Celia responds.

"I don't think he's had to tell her much about my past, though she was blown away by my research on a deal they refused with some players I knew from long ago."

"You and Jake have become good friends, and work partners. I think it's wonderful, the way he trusts you."

"Jake's a gamer. He's been willing to learn the tough lessons and maintain his core goodness. He knows the game but knows when to step back as well. Plus, he's not greedy, and he and Marie are so decent. He never forgets that."

"Leroy, I'm really proud of you. Thanks for being my friend."

"You got it. Thank you for allowing me to fix your camera that day."

*

Delores could feel she was getting sicker. Her joints ached in places that were new, and her stamina had become compromised. She didn't want to tell Arthur how bad she was feeling, but she didn't want to be alone with this pain either. He had just returned from China after a round of fund raising to support a venture he had explored and thought had great promise. He spent an extra day there to discuss with backers the financial arrangements, and if other partners would be involved. There were issues that were not resolved, and he would be required to return in a few weeks. Delores had recently stopped traveling with him, so they were not together as often. When he got home, he came to the bedroom to greet her, but then took a call from Cynthia Tucker that lasted for twenty minutes. He came back, but she had fallen off to sleep. He kissed her forehead gently and went back to his office.

*

"Jake, do you think he's scheming us?" Cynthia asked at lunch.

"I guess his history seems to be just on the edge sometimes. There's never been a question of impropriety, just methodology, I think. He's pretty sharp and has moved the needle in certain areas of financing deals, but everyone says watch him," Jake responds.

"I had a long talk with him last night and expressed our concerns. Now that he has some backing from China, it could go either way. I'm not sure what he's having to give up?" she presents.

"If it's actual product, that's one thing, if it's receivables, I'm still not sure we want to play," Jake says. "How about his moves into heath care insurance?"

"I think that's what the outside money is really about," Cynthia responds.

"Do you think he's a gambler?" Jake asks.

"Of course, but not foolish. He knows how to hedge his bets," she observes.

"Is there anything else?" Jake asks her.

"No, what can we learn?"

*

Leonard was feeling better about things. He was getting a glimpse of what the counselor said about becoming less high over time. The changes were very subtle in perception, and how he thought about what he thought about. His memory was improving as he could recall events of the past year that had been hazy notions about his work and his life with Susie. He was enjoying their walks together, the cats, and not working. Eventually he wanted to get into something part time, but right now he was experiencing a freedom that was long overdue. The freedom to think, and breathe, and just be a human being without the push pull of corporate demands. He was feeling that until he turned on the computer and received a message to refresh or delete a certain file. It was from the runner he had downloaded to his personal devices that contained communications between David and Arthur. He hit the refresh button, and read the three pages:

"David, please tell the doctors that Mr. Rubin has the money. Also, mention to the director that his charity will receive the promised amount. She is drifting further away, and my heart is breaking. The expedited approval will not only help us, but thousands of patients immediately. The public will want to know that. Thank you. Arthur."

Bank Transfer # 38763210 $500,000.00; $600,000.00; $290,000.00 Complete 10:00am EST, May17, 2015. Signed MS.

LF $2mil. Sent. AD JR $4mil. Did not do. AD

Leonard could not remember seeing this before, or why he had gotten it. It took him two days to recall when David had given him the runner as a tool to direct and record payments from debtors. It was a level of redundancy installed several years ago, to help with financial disputes. Leonard was not sure what to do now with this information, they had retired him. He figured he'd save it just in case something was wrong.

*

It had rained all night and hadn't let up when Randall woke at 5:30. He knew he had to square this business for Cyrus, but he was running out of options. The Bureau of Prisons said it was an accident. All security footage was clean, with no unusual activity by any staff members. How he was poisoned was a mystery for them as well, and they rather wished Mr. Brewer, Attorney at Law, would let it rest, and move on. Cyrus had not made any more political noise, until recently, and the Director was expecting another call at any time, probably from the executive branch. It came on a Wednesday.

"Derek, Franklin. How are you?"

"I was doing all right."

"I know. Is there anything else to be reported about the matter?"

"Are we secure?"

"Yes."

"A toxin was found on his left shoe, Clostridium Botulinum."

"Do I share this or let it ride?"

"Ride."

"So, it was an accident?"

"Yes."

The president confided with Cyrus and told him it was confirmed as accidental. Cyrus accepted the report from his old friend, and died a week later, natural causes, old age.

CHAPTER ELEVEN

"Mary, it's Celia. How are you?"

"Celia, so good to hear from you. Thanks for calling, I've been thinking of you and Leroy," Mary says to her.

"Good, we're back on the island for a few weeks. We need to get together," Celia mentions. "When's a good time?"

"Most any time. I'd love to show you some of my paintings!" Mary shares.

"Day after tomorrow, lunch, 11:30?" Celia asks.

"Sounds great, come on over," Mary responds.

"See you then darling."

"Okay love, bye."

Mary thought to return to this morning's acrylic abstract of the marshes behind her house but sat instead in the living room. She started thinking of all that business with Bruce, and what an awful year and a half she's had, living with the pain of his deceptions, and how close she could have been to physical harm. He was a monster, and she never saw it until the end.

Leonard did not want to go to counseling today. He was feeling restless, and otherwise disturbed by the information he uncovered. He wasn't sure what it all meant, or if he had a role in it somehow. He was getting an understanding of what the counselor had told him, that he had been unconscious a long time, and there were huge gaps in his memory about events and actions. He knew he was being paid well, and the work was not that difficult, but were there areas of wrongdoing by company officials, particularly Mr. Davis, and was he a part of it? Was there something he needed to find out before it found him? He thought he needed to give David a call, but he wasn't sure what he would ask him. He started to feel paranoid and decided he did need to go to counseling.

*

"Arthur, per Joe. Docs have signed off on trial data. Director has career fears. Decision tomorrow. It may take more $$$. David."

David had mistakenly left his computer screen open, and Deborah saw the message.

"What's that?" she asked him when he returned from the restroom, pointing to his PC.

"Video game note," he lied to her.

"What's it called, Corruption?" she asked, trying to make a joke, but quickly realizing David wished she had not seen the e-mail.

"No, well, I don't think it, can you forget you saw it?" he asked her, sitting down at his station, looking around the open office space, scanning the three cubicles placed throughout the large room, the usual occupants away for lunch.

"Okay, done," she replies.

"What are you doing after work?" David asks her.

"Not much, home, dinner, listen to some music, you know, work week, 40s single," she says.

"Would you consider joining me for dinner, we can go over some plans I have about workflow changes?" he presents to her.

"Right after, or do I have time to go home and change into something nice?" she asks him.

"Yeah, nice, sure. I'll pick you up about six," he gives her.

"Good, thanks. See you then," she replies to him.

David gets to her apartment building about ten of six, parks, and reads an e-mail note from Joe.

"We're in the house. Meds ready in two days." He then sends a text message to Arthur who responds, "Thank You."

*

Deborah looks outside her fourth-floor unit and sees David's car parked near the fire lane. She checks her hair and make-up, exits her apartment, and takes the elevator down to the ground floor. The doorman greets her, and she strides towards the waiting car, feeling like a schoolgirl on a second date. David gets out of the car and comes around to open the door for her. She gushes and primly sits, smiling seductively and says, "Thank you." David returns to the other side of the car, gets in, smiles at her as she leans towards him and gives him a warm kiss to the mouth. They look at each other and acknowledge they're not hungry for food, and he puts the car in a proper spot, and they go up to her place. They have sex and discuss the particulars of what Deborah had seen on his computer.

They drove over to Washington Park. It was a fair, winter's day and jackets were necessary. They walked a bit, then settled on a bench overlooking the baseball field.

"The dark side, how do you deal with it?" Leroy asked his older brother.

"It's not easy, especially with what we've known. Any particular event?" Larry asks him.

"That whole business with Bruce Walker, and my second stint in prison. It all seems so unnecessary now. Maybe even stupid."

"Using today's knowledge on yesterday's decisions?"

"Well, that, but moreover, why?"

"That's the great mystery to it all. Do you want to go religion, psychology, or philosophy?"

"Religion."

"What I believe is that we have a pre-set purpose, and how we carry it out is up to us. The power, whatever one believes, allows certain acts, and we mold something good from it. Now, to your premise, the darkness. One should accept certain limits to behavior, but if not given proper guidance early in life the unacceptable becomes the known, or prevalent. And we can go down the list, from mildly distasteful to depraved. Your path has led to salvation. I've known a type of retribution, an evening of scores. You were broken, I was empowered. You've had to fight history, me, the present. We both were given skills to survive, and yet, honor a sort of Grace bestowed upon us. You have Celia, I have my work."

"Psychology?"

"Now we get into the particulars! Let's walk a bit," Larry offers. "You see, this has to address the human condition, the uncontrollable, rather, what was given at birth. On the one hand Bruce Walker performed a lot of great technical work, and helped the good guys win, or at least better protect themselves."

"How do you mean?"

"That device, it augmented human decision making in life threatening situations. But he allowed his desire for power and domination to overrule decency. He was a psychopath. Therapy was not going to help him. He kept it together for a long time, because of family connections, and a good foundation. He could not overcome a certain mental twist, and that's the task for all of society, to correct the depths of errant drives."

"How was it that he was able to stay married to Mary?" Leroy asks.

"Remember, he married late in life. He needed her to calm him down, but she could not help him expunge, or rather, separate himself from his psyche. He was times two for good, or evil. He did good, but evil won out in the end. In healthy people, it's the other way around."

"Was he evil, or just sick?"

"He was evil. Sickness speaks to a potential for restoration to health. Once he crossed the line there was no coming back," Larry shares.

"Medication?" Quizzes Leroy.

"Would have made him worse, stronger in his malevolence," Larry responds.

"Emotional redirection?"

"Not possible; he could not feel the remorse?" Larry gives him.

"Philosophy?"

"Now to your main problem, the meaning of things. Your life's pattern has little meaning, that is, you should not have the history you have. But you have it. It's caused you pain and sorrow, and yet, you're doing a lot of good now. Some would argue that you've had these experiences, and that meaning is secondary. I'm not sure. The meaning is in the experience. One has to find it," Larry teaches.

"And how about the soul?" questions Leroy.

"Ha. Most people think it's in the spiritual, or religious, but it's really here. Ones' beliefs lead to experiences with meaning. That's why you can't touch it, but you know it."

"Thus, the dark has its own meaning?"

"Yes?"

CHAPTER TWELVE

Jake and Cynthia were still at odds over the $750 million investment with SixFive Global. The more they talked Jake could sense an emotional strain in her voice that was unusual for this level of financing. Usually she talked data, price points, Wall Street values, declining revenue, decreases in values, long term outlook. Her word choices now were more clinical as she talked of trials, adverse reactions, rapid growth, and malignancies, primary and secondary issues. Was she talking about making money, or was something else at the core of her line of questioning?

"Cynthia, tell me what's going on?" Jake asked her.

"You never met him, and I know I told you the marriage didn't work out, but the reality is he died of cancer a year after we married. Acute Myeloid Leukemia, it developed rather quickly," she shares with him. "All this talk about the efficacy of certain drugs, and Arthur's prospects have left me raw, even though it was eight years ago. Maybe it's not right for us, now. Money is money, but maybe I should stay out of this one?"

"Well, let's have him in, and see what they've got. It may lead us to more health-related investments later if this doesn't work out. There's a tremendous upside to being 'in the field,' so to speak," Jake offers.

"What time tomorrow?" she asks him.

"Eleven thirty-five."

"Why the five?"

"It was a misprint, and Leroy didn't change it."

"Oh."

The more Arthur read, the more discouraged he became. The doctors had not helped him feel better either talking of intracranial neoplasm, failure of differentiation, uncontrollable growth. Treatment was not working, and it was harder on him to watch Delores become more listless, and not recognize him all the time. She was drifting away, but he was glad his efforts would have the home treatments made available soon and she could get better. He was betting on a miracle because she deserved one.

*

Celia and Mary arrived at the beach about one after eating lunch. It was early summer hot, but not sweaty hot. They were enjoying each other's company, and conversation was easy. Mary had come out earlier this morning, looking up at the wisps of streaking, red-pink clouds just ahead of the sun. She felt quite fortunate to have the experience, to live here, and enjoy the island lifestyle. It was moments like those, however, that she missed having someone to share them with and cried a little as she watched couples stroll, hand in hand, or just together, talking, and even the ones with phones, each in a separate world, yet together on a journey of freedom, hopefully the cares of everyday life at a distance.

Celia noticed the far-away look in Mary's eyes when they set up camp near the water, at morning tide's border.

"Where are you?" Celia asked.

"Off in the distance, the iron wheels' roll, the after hum of where it's going," she quotes from a poem by her favorite author.

"That's pretty heavy sister for the beach!" Celia observes.

"I know, I came out this morning, and watching the couples got to me a little," Mary responds.

"Have you met anyone down here, or are you dating at all?" Celia asks her.

"You know, here or there. No one exciting yet," Mary says to her. "One guy died two days after we went out. They assured me it was not my fault, however," she laughs.

"Gallows humor!"

"I know, poor fellow. Sixty-four. Heart attack."

"Did you have him over?"

"No. We hadn't gotten that far."

"Too bad, would have made a great story."

"Oh well, more will be revealed."

"Well, that's true."

"How's Leroy?"

"He's great. Working more, almost full time again. He's flying to China next week," Celia shares.

"China, wow. Are you going?"

"I was invited, but no."

"You're kidding?"

"Just no desire."

"Something wrong?"

"Oh no. Just the long flight. We went to Australia a year ago, for vacation. That was great. We had a chance to fly up then, but I did not want to."

"Reason?"

"I just didn't want to. Really that's it. No buzz."

"Okay. What are you painting these days?"

"More abstracts lately. Fun!"

"You know, I'm sick of the marshes, maybe I need another theme?"

"Do you like the desert?"

"Haven't given it much thought."

"I'm going to Arizona in a few weeks, maybe you can join me. New scenery, new visions?"

"I need to think about that. You may be on to something. You know, sign me up! One of those great Bed and Breakfast places out there. Okay, cool. Let's do it!"

"Okay, that a girl. Let's get you loosened up."

*

"Jake, Leroy."

"Hey buddy, what's up?"

"Did you know Mr. Arthur Davis's wife is dying of cancer?" Leroy asks him.

"How did you find that out?" Jake asks.

"Here, the Wind Chase Stock auction. One of your former employees is living in Quo Chow and told me to tell you hello. She said she did some research for them, and the two cancer drugs have issues. She said they should not have been approved in America. The trials were shortened, and several patients regressed. She thinks they could have worked out the discrepancies over time, maybe in another year, but the lead doctor felt they were ready, especially in severe cases, where they have had success. There were contingencies put in place, but many feel the process was rushed. Dr. Taylor felt she owed you one, especially after I told her the amount of investment we were about to make," Leroy tells him.

"Anything else?" Jake asks him.

"She says Arthur was a frequent guest here over the past year, and may have spread money around to win friends, if you know what I mean?"

"Is he the principle in Wind Chase?"

"58%. $2.3 billion in cash."

"We were not sure, but that's the figure we had."

"Have you all gotten into bed with him yet?"

"No, we were not too far along in the discussion. Boy, this is good and bad news. It confirms what Cynthia had discovered."

"I did have to spend some money, but I do have copies of the research data and reports that were sent out for peer review prior to approval."

"Could it hurt our friend?"

"Not from her. We just talked, but she led me to the person who gave me the data."

"Totally the real deal?"

"Totally."

"Okay, thank you. See you when you get back."

"Roger that."

*

Arthur and Delores were in love, and everyone could see it whenever they were around them. They held hands, pecked each other on the cheek in public, and generally only had eyes for each other. Whether they were at a function, or just out for a meal the intensity of the attraction was obvious and quite endearing. Even their service staff, at home, would light up in their company as the air would be filled with love. When travelling, they did things for each other like teamwork and knew when to help and when to back off a bit. Arguments were average in forcefulness, and disagreements moved away like the tide as they always came back to, "Let's start over."

*

Delores could feel the changes in her body chemistry about six months before the diagnosis. Little pings of pain became more pronounced, and her energy level decreased slowly over time. She became more aware of her forgetfulness and cried in silence the first time she did not recognize Arthur after he returned from a week-long business trip. Of course, what was most awful was the news that the doctor gave her that not much could be done, and that she probably had four months to live. They both gave a look of terror as the thought of them not being together became more real, and the potential devastating effects of disease progression, and what would be necessary to keep her comfortable. It was just unthinkable, and Arthur vowed to her, and more pointedly to himself, to do whatever he could to make her okay.

CHAPTER THIRTEEN

Randall Brewer was coming to believe he needed to let go of his resentment towards Leroy Fleming. Bruce walker was involved in the war on drugs, and there were lots of casualties, and friendships were forged that should not have been. Bruce became corrupted and twisted by the work, as well as his old partner, Thomas Robinson. Leroy understood the players, he met them while in prison, and he understood the depths as well to which the soul gets compromised in those kinds of interactions. The fact was something had gotten lost in Randall's desire to exact a payment from Mr. Fleming. A payment that was not due. Randall was coming around to the fact that Bruce Walker died in a prison cell, period. Accident or not, it was time to let this sleeping dog lie. Nothing good would come out of actions on his behalf. Reality is, Bruce did a lot of good, tough work for the country, and he did a lot of bad in the community. Maybe there is no balance, but it should be over. Randall thought all this until James Freeman called.

"Mr. Brewer, it's James Freeman. How are you today?"

"You know, I'm good, thanks. Going by your real name these days?" Randall says to him, sarcastically.

"Real is why I called sir. Real information."

"You know Charles, that sounds better to me, but you should not call me again. We said our goodbyes a month ago."

"I don't feel like I finished the job for you, sir. I can do that now. I know how Mr. Fleming killed Bruce Walker."

Randall hesitated a minute before he spoke.

"It's a done issue as far as I'm concerned, my man. You can take it somewhere else. The feds may want to talk to you, but I don't."

"Okay, see you around. Can't blame an old con for trying."

*

Their house was rather modest for their means, 5,000 square feet. Of course, having the pool and landscaped garden made for more freedom to roam. They enjoyed alone or together and didn't have a need for over stimulation. Peace and comfort were valued. They enjoyed symphonic concerts, high-brow art exhibits, classical story books, and occasional good, commercial fiction. He enjoyed the murder mysteries, she favored romance, with a little drama. Neither would be called an extrovert, but they enjoyed their commitments to charitable events. Arthur's work forced him to entertain various types of people, but he never stayed longer than necessary to win over a confidence. He was well read, and could make general conversation, but one had to be of a certain mind to keep him engaged. He wanted to close a deal and move on. Their net worth was somewhere north of 3.5 billion, but to walk around the house and grounds one would have guessed a lot less. A half billion or so was what David and Deborah guessed when they were invited over for dinner. Despite the size of contracts David oversaw, and SixFive Global being a privately held company, they just had no clue how well Arthur had managed his business affairs. The house workers were so cordial and easy going, David and Deborah felt at home upon entering.

"Deborah, would you like more cabbage?" Arthur asked her.

"No, thank you, sir, this is excellent," she responds.

"David, anything else?" Arthur asks him.

"More peas please, how did they did this?" he asks.

"An old, family recipe," Arthur shares.

After everyone finishes eating, and sipping on their beverage of choice, Arthur invites his employees to the den for some business-related conversation. After everyone found a seat Arthur began a questioning they did not expect.

"Why have you two found it necessary to go behind my back and deal with discards?" he asks rather forcefully. "And founding your own company, what is that about?" he further asks.

"We needed future planning, divorced from SixFive," David speaks up.

"Yes, we're trying to make our own way," Deborah says to him. "Everything we've done has been totally separate from SixFive. Even some of our clients don't make the connection. So much is automated. They asked for a second look, we had cash."

"And Leonard?" Arthur asked.

Again surprised, David speaks up.

"After he was fired from Global, we terminated our relationship with him as well, and returned his investment, plus a nice bonus. He was happy."

"So where does this go now?" Arthur asks them.

"We would like to stay around, but if now is the time to break, we're ready," Deborah answers.

"Yes, now is the time. Return, or leave all SixFive references, devices, etc. at the office by 10:00am tomorrow. Of course, you know you will be monitored for the next three months by my security staff," Arthur gives them.

"Yes, we understand," they respond in unison.

"Is there anything we need to discuss to keep this civil?" Arthur asks them.

"No. It will be a clean break. We have no issues that would cause you worry," David says.

"The 'runners'?"

"They will be left on the devices. You can clean them later. You may want to review them."

"Leonard?"

"I did not give him one, and I don't think he figured it out," David tells Arthur.

"Okay, fair enough. Good luck to the both of you."

"Thank you, sir. Goodbye," they both say to him.

One of Arthur's house workers comes to the den door, opens it, and ushers them out. They get up, nod towards Arthur, and exit, quietly.

CHAPTER FOURTEEN

Leonard was about ninety days free of marijuana use. He was feeling great, he and Susie were spending a lot of time together, and all was sweet. He was going through old paper files in the garage and found one labeled 'Stocks.' He opened it and read off a list of prime stock certificates that after he checked their current trading values came close to 2.5 million dollars. Half were in his name and half belonged to Susie. He was flabbergasted. His appointment with the counselor was two hours away so he called Susie at work.

"Can you talk?" he asked her.

"Sure, for a few minutes. Let me get away from the desk," she answered. Susie worked as an auditor for an insurance firm and could manage her time as need be. "What's up doc?" she said playfully.

"I was just out in the garage and found a folder with some stock certificates in it. I checked the exchanges and they're worth about 2.5 million. Half in my name and half in your name. Do you know about these?" he asked her, completely puzzled.

"Oh yeah, you bought them for us last year with a bonus Arthur gave you. You thought it was excessive, but he said you had made the company a lot of money. You don't remember?" she says to him.

"No, I don't?" he says to her.

"You have been smoking a lot of dope, haven't you? You don't remember?"

"I really don't. It may come back to me, but I don't remember now."

"Yeah, we put them up, and you used to follow the market sometimes, but you said you lost interest. It was our nest egg, so we just knew it was there."

"Yeah, wow, okay. I guess we'll go to the broker one day."

"Sure, we can do that. I have all the statements you know. I guess you don't remember the oral sex either?"

"When?"

"The day you got the bonus. You said it was the best ever."

"I don't remember."

After a pause, they both give out the greatest laugh ever.

"It'll come back to you," she says.

"I hope so," he says.

They laugh some more, then hang up.

*

No one really talked to Joe Rubin unless they had to, it was always a chore. He just lied and schemed all the time. Arthur had placed a call to him, and it took several hours for Joe to get back to him.

"Mr. Davis, que pasa?"

"Where are you?"

"Can't say. Talk to me."

"How about the principal investigator?"

"The protocols were in order. Once the reports are out everything should be okay. He'll get some heat for stopping testing earlier than projected, but since the meds work all is well," Joe says to him.

"Well thank you."

"My pleasure."

Arthur hangs up the phone and said a prayer that no one gets hurt in all this. He just wanted Delores to get better. He didn't realize he was being recorded.

*

Arthur's former workout room, on the main floor of the house, facing east, was converted into a hospital grade treatment room for Delores. It was bright and comfortable with adequate spacing for her bed, a lounge chair, machines, testing equipment, and a desk for the nurses and doctors to use. Delores was vaguely aware of what was going on, and seemed rather amused by it all, especially when Arthur would visit, and they would talk before she drifted off to sleep. She recognized him half the time now and knew him as the kind man who came to see her. Even though his heart was breaking he would read poetry to her, gesturing as the words dictated, making sure to maintain eye contact, and smile, even when she tilted her head away, he would still look to see if she were okay. It was a deep hurt, for a deep love, hoping for the best.

*

Dr. Joyce Taylor was back from her work in China and contacted Jake Austin to request a luncheon with Cynthia Tucker. It was arranged and they met at the Fish Center on Owl Street. Even though it was raining they both were fresh from their use of limousine service. Each wore tasteful and professional clothing, but nothing showy, and just enough jewelry to state, "I have more, but you can enjoy these trinkets this afternoon."

The restaurant was full of middle-aged business owners, and other upper-level executives. There was just enough buzz to acknowledge wealth, education, and power to effect change. No one looked around much but stayed focused with whomever they were with. Occasionally someone of high note would be singled out in greeting, or a goodbye, but generally the room was full of equals. There was a smell of fish prepared without seasoning, pure and healthy, and one would get their portion, and savor what seemed like this morning's catch. The aroma filled the air and made the setting inviting and comfortable. If one were not careful, one might make a deal that would need to be tweaked, later on. As their plate of white fish arrived with cheese bread and vegetables, and a small amount of white wine offered if one were inclined to embellish the meat just a bit, Dr. Taylor spoke to why she wanted to meet.

"Cynthia, thank you very much for joining me for lunch. Jake was gracious in responding to my call, and I appreciate you taking the time to meet with me."

"Of course, Jake was glad to hear from you, and that things are working out well for you. He did mention a little history about your work," Cynthia starts.

"Well, he's a great guy. So decent."

"That he is."

"I don't know how much, if any, information he's given you about my work with Wind Chase, but bad winds are shifting there," Joyce offers.

"Yes, he did update me, and we decided not to play with them," Cynthia responds.

"Quite sad about Arthur."

"How do you mean?"

"The indictments."

"What indictments?"

"Corruption allegations."

"In China, or here?"

"Here. FDA."

"Oh dear, poor Arthur. Do you have any details?"

"I can't say much because of my work for them in China," Joyce gives her.

"Yeah, that's right," Cynthia agrees.

"Well, at any rate, the reason I requested to meet with you is that I am looking to do more work."

"In your field?"

"Possibly."

"Start a business?"

"Not so much, but more consulting to businesses."

"How?"

"Genetics And Group Representation: Diversify Your Workforce with Genetic Coding."

"That's curious? Where do we come in?"

"As a tester. How diversified are you, and how does it matter?"

"Whoa. I didn't expect this?"

"No, as a privately held concern is it relevant for you to have a formula?"

"Mmmnn. In house, or with our vendors?"

"Both."

"This calls for another meeting. My office next week or so?"

"Yes. I'll call with some dates and times."

"I like it. Thanks."

"Sure. Thank you."

*

"Larry, what's up my man?" spoke Leonard, smiling, as he came into the office.

"Boy, you are feeling better," Larry comments.

"Yes, I am! This clean living is good. I wanted to ask you two things, one, do we always have to meet here in the office, and two, should we have Susie come in for a family type session?"

"No and yes. We can go out for coffee or lunch, and yes, only where the relationship has been hurt by the using. From what you've shared you all seem to have a great relationship," Larry responds.

"Twenty-three years, it's been great. She did mention it, though."

"Yeah, have her come in; she can tell me where the money is hidden," Larry says jokingly.

"Funny you should say that. You know how we've talked about the memory loss, or lack, or non-existence in some cases, well, I was going through some files and found stock certificates that I didn't remember anything about. Susie did, however. It was a sizable amount, and I still do not recall the transaction. I mean a lot of money," Leonard shares.

"Smoking dope! Well, it won't harm you, right?"

"You're preaching to your newest choir member you know!"

"I know, it's amazing, and everyone's experience is different. I was doing a lot of other drugs as well, so I went pretty far out there. Marijuana was not my first choice, but if I was getting high, I was going to smoke some weed too. It took me eighteen months to concentrate long enough to read a novel again, once I got clean. And of course, there are hundreds of events I have no recollection of, which sounds odd, but it's just that I was high every day, and something was happening with folks, or by myself, but there's a lot I don't remember!"

"You too?"

"Absolutely, so you're right on schedule."

"Okay, good, maybe I'll find some more money?"

"Or you may find out you owe someone!"

"God forbid!"

"Okay, see you next week."

"Same time, same bat station?"

"You got it."

CHAPTER FIFTEEN

"Jake, you seem moody this evening?" Marie asked him after dinner.

"I'm in a quandary. I want to take the lecturer role at the college. H.U.N. is just not working out. I'm having a been there, done that experience. I think it's over."

"Have you talked to Cynthia?"

"Not yet, but when I fly out next week, I'll mention it to her."

"Do you think she'll try and talk you out of it?"

"She's pretty sharp, she may already sense it?"

"How about Leroy?"

"I'll call him tomorrow; he'll probably do, whatever."

"What do you mean?"

"Leroy is a fascinating guy, and Cynthia would be lucky to have him stay around. I'm the changeable part. He's special."

"So, Professor Austin?"

"I think so."

"What will you tell the kids?"

"Let's have a general talk, and see where they stand? I'd be curious to hear what they have to say."

"I am too. We have such a good life. I think this is a good move for you."

"Right you are."

*

"Arthur, Harvey. Boy, I don't hear good things," his oldest and best friend says to him.

"What are you hearing?" Arthur asks.

"Ah man, the FDA, what have you done over there?"

"Harvey, slow down, what's happening?"

65

"Your name is being thrown around in closed circles related to a corruption investigation," Harvey shares with him.

"What do you mean?"

"Arthur, a Joe Rubin was arrested yesterday, and he signed documents implicating you as an agent of large money to sway a decision on the length of a drug investigation. He says you paid him to have doctors say a drug was ready for approval, six months prematurely. He says he has dates, times, money transfers, all that."

"Harvey, do we need to go on with this conversation, or can we meet in about an hour?"

"Arthur, handle your business, I can't say any more."

*

Arthur administered the evening dose at 6pm. Delores was awake, but in a dream-like state of awareness. She mumbled a thank you to him, but they both knew that the medication had not stopped the advance of her disease. She went to sleep, and Arthur sat with her for an hour. He was glad she was not in pain, for surely this process would have been unbearable if she were. He had spent tremendous sums of money over the past 14 years to develop drugs to help mankind, and surely, he did not know that one day it would be the love of his life who would need them the most. He was remorseful now that his efforts to beat a natural deadline had failed, his tears were full, and difficult. He told her that he loved her and that all would be well. Even in her compromised state of consciousness she smiled, and then went into a coma. The medical personnel came about 9 o'clock and she was transferred to a specialized facility to further care for her needs. Arthur drove to their 17th floor apartment near his office building, and within twenty minutes jumped to his death.

*

Jake could not understand why the two men were following him and Marie. They were in one of the premier shopping malls in the country and those guys seemed out of place. They were dressed in standard, nice guy garb, but something about the way they passed by the second time, and stared Marie down gave him pause. If it were a standard robbery attempt, he would give them the watch, and three pairs of slacks, but, if they wanted more there was going to be an issue.

At first Jake thought to go by way of the food court, then to the parking garage, but decided he would know immediately if they also left this floor using the elevator. He mentioned their warning code word, and Marie easily put her left hand into her purse to secure the pistol. By then the men had gone another way and Jake and Marie felt relieved.

*

Jake and Leroy left H.U.N. Ltd. to pursue general investing as a sideline to their other interests. They each put up $20 million to a fund and started researching businesses to help get off the ground. They would pursue some unconventional routes and see what they came up with. They had asked Larry to join them, but he said he liked to let his money sit and do nothing, which wasn't true since he had picked some stocks back in the early 2000s that were outperforming the markets.

"That was a curious state of affairs," Jake said to Leroy when they had the first official business meeting in the new office space they had leased. "Cynthia is a friend, but that was just not a good fit for us, too much money drives some people crazy!"

"Yeah. That whole thing with Arthur Davis, boy, sad, but where was his ethics training?" Leroy asked his partner.

"I'm not sure which was primary, that, or the emotion of his wife's illness," Jake responds. "As the song goes, 'love will make you do wrong!' But of course, it can make you do right as well."

"What do you think about Joyce Taylor?" Leroy asked him.

"Business or personal?" Jake asks him.

"Everything," Leroy pushed.

"I don't know. She's doing some good work, but I just don't know her," Jake pondered.

"Maybe you do, and there's not much there?" Leroy offers.

"Oh no, there's a lot there, I'm not sure if we would want her around? She did credible work for WES, and then we went back and forth about what she wanted to do afterwards. Seems like she's found it now as a consultant to the healthcare industry, she is a scientist, after all," Jake goes on about her.

"She's a strange woman and I thought It odd she would show up where we were," Leroy presents.

"Yeah, coincidence, fate, I don't know. Leroy, when you assess your life, what comes up?" Jake asks.

"That's a great question! On the one hand, everything that's happened seems so outrageous, yet there's a logical progression to it all. Being in prison all those years, getting a degree, working with the youth center, meeting Celia in the middle of nowhere, and the fact that I was there, it's all strange. Then, going back to prison, and all that, well, interesting," Leroy shares.

"Why did you go back to prison?" Jake earnestly asks him.

"Oh, I thought you knew? That's the strangest part, hooking a friend up to buy some dope, crazy, and he was a snitch, which I understand because he wanted to get out of some trouble. The rest of it, the players, I guess that's the worst of it. It's old news now, but those rogue government boys, that, was nuts. And I guess that's where the whole Dr. Taylor thing comes to mind, her, and Bruce Walker, crazy?"

"Weren't you and Bruce kind of friendly at one point?" Jake asks him.

"Man, I don't know. Friendly is not the term though," Leroy shares. "You see, they had something on an acquaintance, a hitman out of Detroit. He contacted me, it's a long story. It was the best acting job of my life. I used Bruce, he used me, but a friend was killed, and they implicated me through some back channels. They sold a lie to the press and moved on. When they went after Larry on a stupid tip at Hobe, I became incredibly angry and pulled some strings of my own. No, we were never friends," Leroy tells him.

"How about Bruce's death?"

"Let's just say older brother outdid younger brother."

Also by George H. Clowers, Jr.

Watch for more at https://www.georgeclowers.com.

About the Author

Retired substance use disorder counselor.
Read more at https://www.georgeclowers.com.

Milton Keynes UK
Ingram Content Group UK Ltd.
UKHW030144051224
452010UK00001B/154

9 798230 290872